Sleepytime Treasury

A Bedtime Tale
for Every Day of the Week

Contents

SIMON & SCHUSTER

This collection first published in Great Britain in 2016 by Simon & Schuster UK Ltd

1st Floor, 222 Gray's Inn Road, London WC1X 8HB

A CBS Company

Little One's Bedtime text copyright © 2011 Suzi Moore / illustrations copyright © 2011 Rosie Reeve

Ping & Pong Are Best Friends (mostly) text and illustrations copyright © 2013 Tim Hopgood

Dogs Don't Do Ballet text copyright © 2010 Anna Kemp / illustrations copyright © 2010 Sara Ogilvie

No-Bot, the Robot With No Bottom text and illustrations copyright © 2013 Sue Hendra & Paul Linnet

Oliver and Patch text copyright © 2015 Claire Freedman / illustrations copyright © 2015 Kate Hindley

The Biggest Kiss text copyright © 2010 Joanna Walsh / illustrations copyright © 2010 Giuditta Gaviraghi

Roo the Roaring Dinosaur text copyright © 2015 David Bedford / illustrations copyright © 2015 Mandy Stanley

The right of David Bedford, Claire Freedman, Giuditta Gaviraghi, Sue Hendra, Kate Hindley, Tim Hopgood, Anna Kemp, Paul Linnet, Suzi Moore, Sara Ogilvie, Rosie Reeve, Mandy Stanley and Joanna Walsh to be identified as the authors and illustrators of this work has been asserted by them in accordance with the Copyright, Designs and Patents Act, 1988

A CIP catalogue record for this book is available from the British Library upon request

978-1-4711-6005-9 (HB)

Printed in China

1 3 5 7 9 10 8 6 4 2

Little One's Bedtime

Suzi Moore and Rosie Reeve

It was late at night and time for bed.
The sky was dark when Somebody said,

"Come, Little One. Little One, come.
It's time to sleep, my Little One."

But Little One grumbled and Little One groaned.
"I'm not even tired," Little One moaned.

"I can't go to bed," Little One said. "Because · · ·

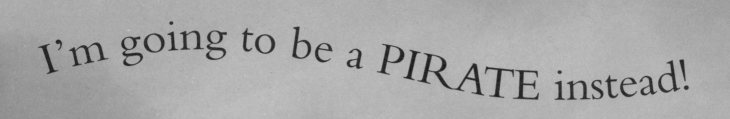

I'm going to be a PIRATE instead!

Come along, Teddy. No time for a nap.
There's gold to be found and I have the map.
Let's sail to the island. I know the way.
We'll find all the treasure. Anchors aweigh!"

It was late at night and time for bed.
   The clock was ticking when Somebody said,

"Come, Little Pirate. Come in from the sea.
   Don't forget Teddy and come up with me."

But Little One stomped and jumped up and down.
"I'm still not tired," she said with a frown.

"I can't go to bed," Little One said. "Because . . .

I'm going to be a MONSTER instead!

Look! I'm a monster with a monstery nose.
I have monstery fingers and monstery toes.
Come along, Teddy! It's going to be great.
Monsters **always** stay up very late."

It was late at night and time for bed.
  The stars were twinkling when Somebody said,

"Come, little monster. Little One, come.
  Into the bathroom, Little One run."

So Little One ran and stood at the sink.
"I have an idea!" she said with a wink.

"I can't go to bed," Little One said. "Because . . .

I'm going to be a KNIGHT instead!

I'll ride to the castle with Teddy the Brave.

There's always a beautiful Princess to save.

Watch out for the dragon! I know what to do.

Excuse me, fierce dragon, it's bedtime for you."

It was late at night and time for bed.

The moon was shining when Somebody said,

"Come, Little One. Little One, come.

It's getting late, my brave Little One."

But Little One jumped and sprang up to run.
Staying up late was always such fun.

"I can't go to bed," Little One said. "Because . . .

I'm going to be a DANCER instead!

I'll dance to the left. I'll dance to the right.

I'm going to be a ballerina tonight.

Come along, Teddy. It's time for the show.

I'm really quite famous or didn't you know?"

It was late at night and time for bed.

The stars were sparkling when Somebody said,
"Come, Little One. Little One, come.

Dance into your bedroom, my beautiful one."

So Little One danced and Little One pranced.
She'd stay up all night if she just got the chance.

"I can't go to bed," Little One said. "Because . . .

I'm going to be a WIZARD instead!

Come along, Teddy! There is magic to make.
Wizards don't sleep! They just stay awake.
I'll magic a rabbit right out of my hat.
I'll turn my big brother into a rat."

It was late at night and time for bed.

The owls were hooting when Somebody said,

"Come, Little One. Little One, come.

It's very late, my magical one.

Don't forget Teddy. Climb up into bed.

No more adventures. It's bedtime instead."

Little One sighed and thought for a while.
"I am a bit tired," she said with a smile.

Under the covers Little One wriggled.
"I'll **dream** of adventure," Little One giggled.

Then Somebody kissed her and turned out the light.
"Sweet dreams, my Little One.

I love you. Goodnight!"

PING & PONG
ARE BEST FRIENDS
(mostly)

Tim Hopgood

Anything Ping can do,

Pong can do better.

Anything?
Yes, anything!

Ping likes ice-skating.

Pong does too!

Ping likes painting.

Pong does too!

Ping likes fishing.

Pong does too!

Now do you see what I mean?

Ping is learning to squeak French.

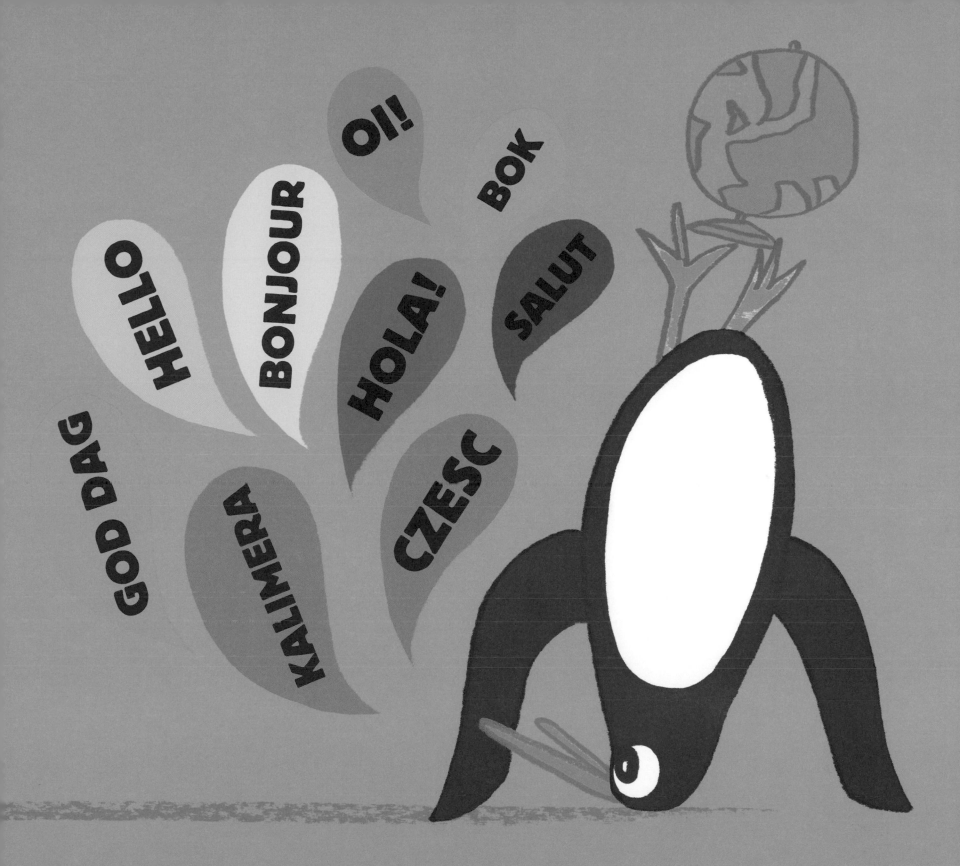

Pong can already squeak in nine different languages.

Ping decided enough was enough.

He was never going to be the **BEST** at **anything**.

So Ping sat down and did **NOTHING**.

"What are you doing?" asked Pong.
"NOTHING," replied Ping.

"Oh!" said Pong.
"I've never tried doing
that before. What do
you have to do?"

"NOTHING," replied Ping.
"Oh, I see," said Pong.

And Pong went off to
practise doing **NOTHING**.

Pong tried as hard as he could,
but he just couldn't do it.

Doing nothing was **IMPOSSIBLE**.

How does Ping do it? he wondered.

Pong decided he didn't like doing nothing.

But doing other things without Ping wasn't much fun.

So he wrote Ping a letter.

Dear Ping,
If you can spare the time,
I wondered if you would
like to come for tea?
I miss you.

Pong x

Ping didn't open the letter straight away.

He was too busy . . .

. . . doing nothing.

Finally Ping read the letter.

He realized he missed his friend too.

The next day,
Ping made some biscuits.

And then he went to visit Pong.

Even though they were a bit burnt,

Pong said they were the nicest biscuits he'd ever tasted.

Pong had also done some baking.

TO THE BEST FRIEND IN THE WORLD

And, at last,
Ping realized he
was THE BEST
at something after all.

DOGS don't do Ballet

Anna Kemp

Illustrated by Sara Ogilvie

My dog is not like other dogs.

He doesn't do dog stuff like weeing on lampposts,
or scratching his fleas, or drinking out of the toilet.

If I throw him a stick,

he looks at me like I'm crazy.

So I have to fetch it myself.

No, my dog likes music and moonlight and walking on his tiptoes.

You see, my dog doesn't think he's a dog . . .

My dog thinks he's a ballerina!

When I get ready for ballet class, he looks longingly at my tutu and ballet shoes and I just know he is dreaming of his name in lights.

"Dad," I say. "Can Biff come too? He loves ballet."
"Not a chance," says Dad. "Dogs don't do ballet!"

Then, one Saturday on my way to class, I get a funny
feeling. A funny feeling that I am being watched.
A funny feeling that I am being followed.

When Miss Polly is teaching us a new routine, I think I see something peeking in at the window. Something with a wet nose. Something with a tail.

"Right girls," says Miss Polly. "Who's going to demonstrate first position?"

But, before anyone can step forward, there is a loud bark from the back of the hall and something furry rushes to the front.

"What is this?" asks Miss Polly, peering over her glasses.

"This," I say, "is my dog."

"Well take it away at once," says Miss Polly,
wrinkling up her nose. "Dogs don't do ballet!"
My poor dog stops wagging his tail and
his ears droop down at the ends.

I take my dog home and give him a bowl of
Doggie-Donuts. But he won't touch them.

He just stays in his kennel for days and
days, and at night he howls at the moon.

For my birthday I get tickets for the Royal Ballet.
"Can Biff come too?" I ask Dad. "He loves ballet."
My dog pricks up his ears and wags his tail.

"No," says Dad. "If I've told you once,
I've told you a thousand times: dogs don't do ballet!"

As we wait for the bus I think about my
poor old dog, all on his own, howling at the moon.
Then I get a funny feeling.

A funny feeling that I am being watched.

A funny feeling that I am not alone.

The ballet is magical!
The orchestra plays as the prima ballerina dances
and prances, and twirls and whirls, and skips and . . .

Oh, no! She trips! Disaster! Calamity!
"It's all over!" I think.

But somebody doesn't think it is over.
No, somebody thinks it is just
beginning. Somebody with
big black eyes, somebody
with pointy ears, somebody . . .

. . . wearing my tutu!

The audience gasps.
"It's a dog!" someone shouts.
"Dogs don't do ballet!"

My dog turns bright red and looks at his feet.
"That's what I've always said," Dad mutters.
But then the orchestra starts to play . . .

. . . and my dog dances like no dog
has ever danced before.
Plié! Jeté! Arabesque! Pirouette!

He is as light as a sugarpuff!
As pretty as a fairy!
The audience can't believe it.
"Hooray!" I shout. "That's my dog!"

When the music stops, my dog
gives a hopeful curtsey and blinks
nervously into the spotlight. The theatre is
so very quiet that you could hear a bubble pop.

Then the lady in the front row stands up.
"It's a dog!" she shouts.
Biff's ears start to droop again.

"A dog that does ballet!" she adds. "Bravo!"
Suddenly the whole audience cheers and throws
bunches of roses. My dog glows pink with happiness.
"I don't believe it," says Dad, shaking his head.
"Biff IS a ballerina after all!"
"See," I say proudly, ruffling Biff's ears,
"Dogs DO do ballet. Bravo, Biff!"

SUGAR PUG FAIRY
TAKES BALLET BY STORM!

NO-BOT

THE ROBOT WITH NO BOTTOM!

Sue Hendra
& Paul Linnet

Bernard the robot loved to play at the park.

Wheeee!
He swung high, high, high,
up into the sky.

Soon it was time to go. Bernard jumped off the swing and headed home.

He'd only walked a little way, when . . .

"My bottom!" cried Bernard.
"It's disappeared! Where can it be?"

Bernard went back to the park to look,
but he couldn't see his bottom anywhere.

"Excuse me, Monkey," he said.
"Have you seen my bottom?"

"Hmmm," said Monkey. "I think I might have.
Bird is using it. Come and see!"

"Hello, Bird," said Monkey. "Have you still got Bernard's bottom?"

"Ooops, Bernard, was that your bottom?" said Bird. "It was too heavy to be a nest . . .

...so I gave it to Bear to use in his drum kit. Let's go and get it back."

"Excuse me, Bear, have you been drumming on my bottom?" asked Bernard.

"Ooops, Bernard, was that your bottom?" said Bear. "It made a funny noise so I couldn't use it. I don't know where it is now."

"Oh," said Bernard.

"Don't worry. Your bottom's got to be somewhere," said his friends kindly.

"Look, there it is!" said Monkey.

"That's just Gary's hat," said Bernard.

"There!" said Bird.

"That's just Edward's shopping basket," said Bernard.

"Isn't that it?" said Bear.
"No, that's just Dog's window box."

Bernard was sad. "I'll never get my bottom back," he sobbed.

"Come and sit down," said his friends,
"and we'll think where to look next."

"I CAN'T sit down!" said Bernard.
"I haven't got a bottom!
I'm not a robot –

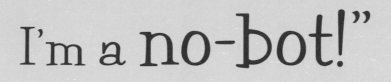
I'm a **no-bot!**"

And he walked away, to carry on looking.

After a while, he arrived at the beach.
He looked out to sea, and saw something
very familiar.

There it was . . .

"Come back!" he shouted. "Come back here! You've got my bottom!" But the rabbits couldn't hear him.

Bernard jumped and waved but it was no good.

Then, as he turned away, he spotted
a strange-shaped sandcastle.

He had found his BOTTOM!

Bernard was so happy to have his bottom back, he did a wiggling, jiggling dance – and so did all his friends!

And Bernard never lost his bottom again.

Oliver had just moved to the big city. It felt strange, and his old home in the countryside seemed far, far away.

"I miss the green fields," Oliver sighed. "I miss the wide open spaces. Most of all, I miss my friends."

One morning, Oliver felt restless. Even though the rain was pouring
down like silver needles, he wanted to be outside, to explore.
People hurried by, un-seeing and un-looking.

Oliver glanced about, wondering which way to go, when suddenly
he saw it, bright as a poppy in a cornfield . . .

. . . a small, soggy, white ball of a dog, trailing a streak of red leash.

He was all alone, just like Oliver.

"Hello!" said Oliver. "Are you lost?"

He looked at the little dog's collar tag. Patch, it read.
Just Patch.

Oliver looked around.

No one was calling for their little lost dog.

"What shall I do with you?" Oliver said to Patch.
"I can't leave you on your own."

Before he knew it, Oliver had the lead in his hand and Patch was trotting along beside him.

Oliver and Patch had a wonderful day
getting to know each other.

For the first time since moving to the city, Oliver felt happy.

But as dusk fell, Patch became
sad. He sat on Oliver's desk
by the window and gazed out
longingly.

Somewhere out there,
in the rain-hazy twinkle
of the city night lights,
was his real home.

Oliver woke the next morning to scratchy, scuffling noises. "Oh, Patch!" Oliver laughed.

They played all day long.

Hide and seek!

Tickle tummy!

Bury the biscuit!

Curl up and cuddle!
(Their favourite.)

Watering the garden –
oops!

But at bedtime Patch seemed sad again.
And even though it made him feel wobbly,
Oliver knew he had to do The Right Thing.

So the next day he made some posters.

He secretly hoped no one
would see them.

FOUND
SMALL WHITE DOG CALLED PATCH
LIKES CHEWING CUSHIONS
LOVES ANYTHING THE COLOUR RED
DOES SOMERSAULTS
TELEPHONE OLIVER 123456789

He stuck up the posters and asked at some shops and houses.

"No, never seen that dog before," the shopkeepers said.

"No one I know is missing a dog," said his neighbours.

Days slipped by and nobody called.

Oliver began to believe that Patch would be his dog forever.

He bought him a cosy red blanket and lots of toys.

It was as if they had always been friends.

One morning, it was gently drizzling.
Oliver and Patch went exploring.
They wandered down a narrow street,
past tall iron railings by an ancient church.
Suddenly, Patch barked.
He tugged hard on the lead and broke free.

"Patch!" Oliver called.
"PATCH!"

Breathless, Oliver reached a tiny park, hidden away like
a jewel. A girl was sitting on the swings, sad and alone.
Oliver looked at her red coat and red boots – and he knew.

The little girl was hugging Patch. Hugging and hugging.
Oliver tried to be brave, but his world had turned grey again.
"Hello, I'm Ruby," the girl said, smiling at Oliver.
"Have you been looking after Patch for me?"

"It's been lovely," said Oliver, trying hard to smile back.
"But I'm really going to miss him."
Then he had a thought. "Ruby, do you think – maybe –
you and Patch would like to visit me one day?"

"We'd love to!" said Ruby. "But why don't we go and do
something together – right now?"
"Woof!" barked Patch. "Woof woof!"
Oliver and Ruby laughed.

At that moment the sun burst out. The pavements shone as a
million raindrops glistened like gold. The city looked beautiful.

And Oliver realised he hadn't lost a friend . . .

. . . he had found another one!

The Biggest Kiss

Joanna Walsh & Judi Abbot

Kisses on noses,

kisses on toes-es.

Sudden **kisses** when you least supposes.

Who likes to **kiss**?

I do! I do! Even the shy do.

Why not try, too?

Frogs like to **kiss,**

and dogs like to **kiss.**

'normous

elephants do.

Little tiny ants do.

Do worms **kiss** underground, with the soil all around?

Do fish **kiss**
like this —

splosh,

splash,

splish?

Some **kisses** are misses,
they land on the ear or near.
But **kisses** with lipstick stick like . . .

a **kiss** with honey,

a **kiss** that's yummy,

a **kiss** on the elbow,

a **kiss** on the tummy.

The rain's **kiss** on your skin is fun.

The snow's **kiss** on your face is ace.

The
TALLEST
kiss is a
tricky kind.

The smallest **kiss** is hard to find.

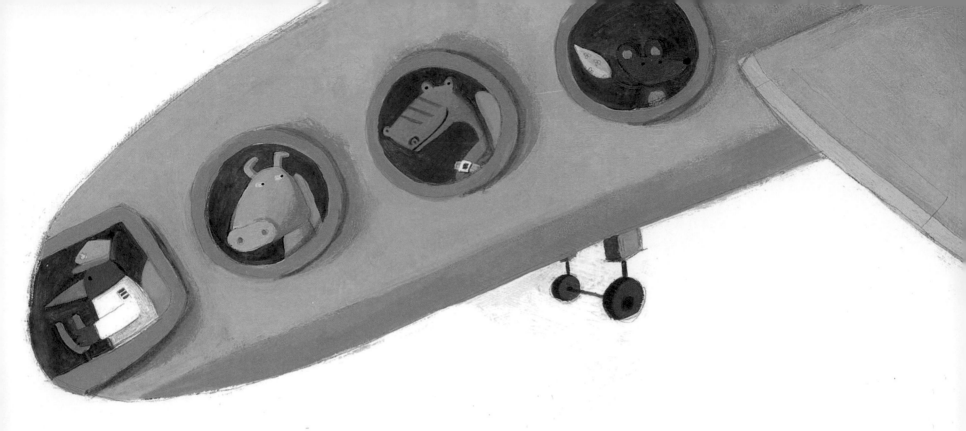

Bye-bye
kisses,

fly-high
kisses,

eye-dry
kisses,

all my
kisses.

I wish for a **kiss** before breakfast,
to start the day right.

And a **kiss** at the end
to say, "Good night!"

I've had all these **kisses,**
and lots more too.

But the very
best kiss . . .

is a **kiss** from you!

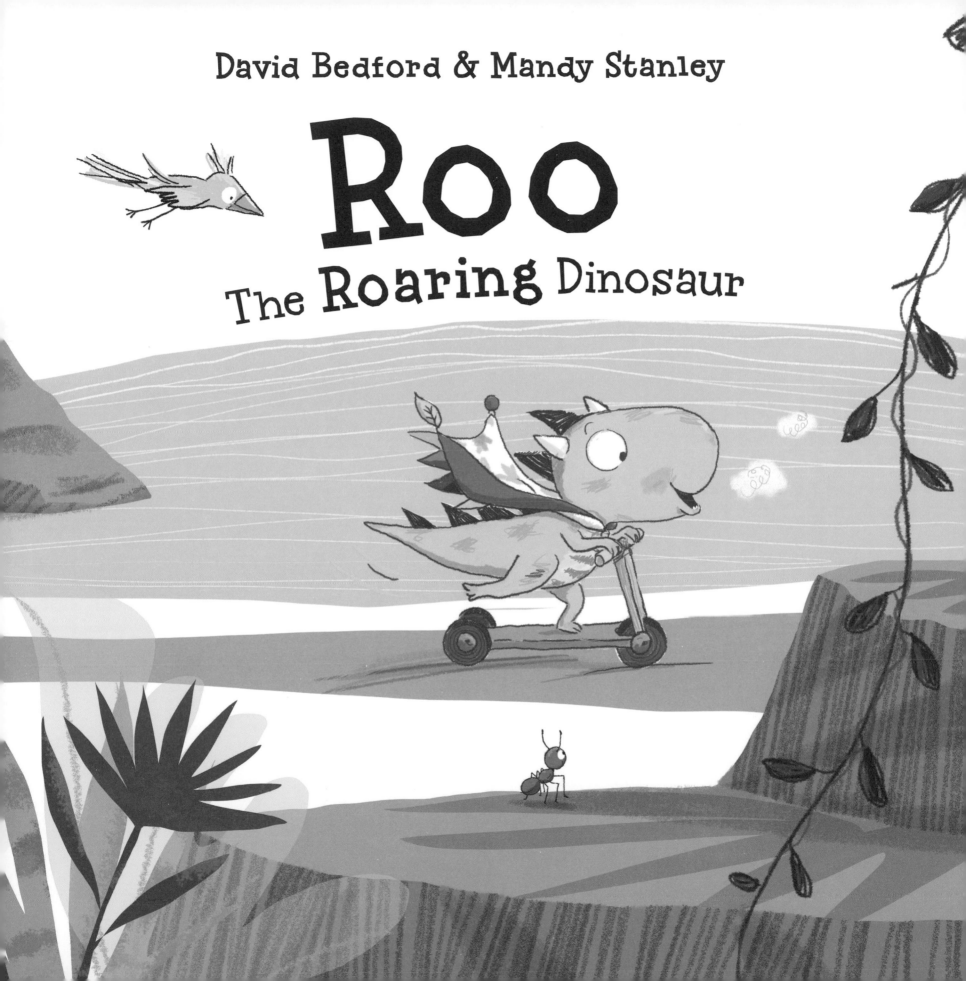

David Bedford & Mandy Stanley

Roo
The Roaring Dinosaur

Roo the Roaring Dinosaur loved his Moomie.
It was Roo's **favourite** thing ever.

Roo and his Moomie always hid from the rain together . . .

and played in the sun together.

Roo never went anywhere without his Moomie.

And wherever his Moomie went,
Roo always followed.

Then one day –

SWOOSH! HISSSS!

It was a flying thing!
Red and blue and big and round.
And it was coming Roo's way!

'Roo run!' said Roo. 'Roo hide!'

Boing,

boing,

A new creature landed - BUMP -
right in front of Roo's nose.

'Oof!'

The new creature looked worried. 'My balloon is broken,' he said.
He looked so sad that Roo decided to do something funny
to cheer him up.

'Play Roo?' he said.

The creature tried a smile. 'All right Roo,' he said.
'I'm Wooly by the way.'

So Roo showed Wooly a
game to play in the sun . . .

and what to do when
the rain came down.

Then Roo took Wooly to . . .

his favourite place.

They sipped tasty coconut coolers.

And had lumpy, bumpy piggy-back rides.

Wooly showed Roo how
to make a camp.

They had supper on sticks
and sang fireside songs.

And when it got dark
they lay on the grass
and watched shooting stars
until they fell asleep.

The next morning Wooly looked sad again. 'I wish I could stay and play but I really do have to go home now,' he said. 'The trouble is, my balloon has a hole in it. And I don't know how to fix it.'

Roo wanted to help. But there was only one thing
that was the right shape and size
to patch up the hole – and it was Roo's!

'Moomie mine!' said Roo. 'No give Moomie.'

Then Roo thought very hard. Moomie belonged to Roo.
But now Wooly needed it more.

So Roo made a very big decision. He hugged his
Moomie one last time. Then 'Give Moomie,' he said.

'Thank you, Roo,' said Wooly. 'You're the best friend ever.'

And together they stitched Moomie over the hole in Wooly's balloon.

But the balloon still wouldn't fly.

'I forgot!' said Wooly. 'It needs lots and lots of hot air.'

And that's when Roo had a brilliant idea.

'ROOOOOOO!'

he roared.

Suddenly the balloon
rose up in the air.
'Now I know why
you're called Roo!'
Wooly laughed.

'Bye, Roo!' he called. 'I won't forget you!'

'Bye!' Roo called back. 'Roo miss you.'

And then, more quietly. 'Bye, Moomie,' he said.

Wooly and the balloon were soon far, far away.

So was Roo's Moomie.

Then suddenly Roo looked up and saw something floating down towards him.

This is for you ROO Love Wooly x

'New Moomie!' roared Roo, happily.

'Roo love new Moomie!'

And off he went to play with his
new favourite thing ever.

The End